Farmer Brown
Goes Round and Round

For my husband, Robert, who sometimes goes in circles —T.S.

For Sarah, Sandy, and Vernon —N.B.W.

SCHOLASTIC INC.
New York Toronto London Auckland Sydney
Mexico City New Delhi Hong Kong

FARMER BROWN
Goes Round and Round

by Teri Sloat

illustrated by Nadine Bernard Westcott

ISBN 0-439-19099-1

Text copyright © 1999 by Teri Sloat.
Illustrations copyright © 1999 by Nadine Bernard Westcott.
All rights reserved.
Published by Scholastic Inc., 555 Broadway, New York, NY 10012,
by arrangement with DK Publishing, Inc.
SCHOLASTIC and associated logos are trademarks and/or registered
trademarks of Scholastic Inc.

12 11 10 9 8 7 6 5 4 3 2 1   1 2 3 4 5/0

Printed in the U.S.A.   14

First Scholastic printing, January 2001

Book design by Chris Hammill Paul.
The text of this book is set in 16 point Stempel Schneidler.
The illustrations for this book were painted in watercolor.

"My chores are done," said Farmer Brown. The air was filled with happy sounds—

A purring cat, a snoring hound . . .
Pigs that oinked,
Cows that moo'd,
Sheep that baa'd,
Doves that coo'd,
Hens that clucked
While donkey brayed,
Goats that naa'd,
A mare that neighed,
His bossy little rooster who
Crowed Cock-A-Doodle-Doodle-Doo!

But then he heard a rumbling sound
That made his smile turn upside down.

Farmer Brown heard thunder drumming.
Lightning flashed; the air was humming.

"Look out!" he cried. "A twister's coming!"

A black cloud raced across the ground.
The twister's tail came dancing down,
And whisked the rooster, cat, and hound
Into the air—with Farmer Brown!

While clouds of sheep swirled through the air,
The clothesline chased the goat and mare
Until each one had on a pair
Of Farmer Brown's plaid underwear!

The twister roared,
The twister grew,
Horns and hooves
And white wool blew
Round snouts and tails
All curly-cued,
While fur and feet
And feathers flew.

Frightened pigs sailed on the backs
Of dairy cows marked white and black.
Hens laid eggs when thunder cracked,
They hit the farmer with a *smack!*

Then, once they all were spinning round,
The wind just stopped . . .
                    and
                            dropped
                                    them
                                            down.

The farmer landed safe and sound. His animals were all around. BUT. . .

His cows oinked,
The pigs moo'd,
His sheep clucked,
The cat coo'd.
The mare howled,
His hens brayed,
The goats meowed,
His hound neighed.
The donkey naa'd
And ate the towel,
The doves baa'd;

The farmer scowled—
"What's wrong with you?" he tried to shout,
But Cock-A-Doodle-Doo came out!

The next thing that the farmer knew,
He heard his bossy rooster, who
Was telling him what HE should do—

"You have to milk the mooing sows,

And slop the muddy, oinking cows.

Go check the nests the sheep have made,
And gather any eggs they've laid!

"Get the shirt the donkey's chewing;

Give birdseed to the cat—he's cooing.

Coo!

Take the baaing doves to pasture—

Feed the hound his oats! Work faster!

"Pet the goats—they keep meowing;
Throw the mare her bone—she's howling!

Hitch the hens up!
Plow the ground."

The rooster frowned. "What *is* that sound?"